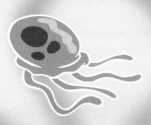

nickelodeon™

SpongeBob
SQUAREPANTS™

Contents

Produced by Downtown Bookworks

DOWNTOWN
BOOKWORKS INC.

President Julie Merberg
Senior Editor Sarah Parvis
Assistant Editor LeeAnn Pemberton
Redesigned by Richman Creative Group
Special Thanks Patty Brown, Pam Abrams

Written by Brenda Apsley and Chloe Martin
Original designs by Graham Wise, Catherine Ellis, Rebecca Studd, and Nick Brown

Time HOME ENTERTAINMENT

Publisher Richard Fraiman **General Manager** Steven Sandonato **Executive Director, Marketing Services** Carol Pittard **Director, Retail & Special Sales** Tom Mifsud **Director, New Product Development** Peter Harper **Director, Bookazine Development & Marketing** Laura Adam **Publishing Director, Brand Marketing** Joy Butts **Assistant General Counsel** Helen Wan **Design & Prepress Manager** Anne-Michelle Gallero **Book Production Manager** Susan Chodakiewicz **Assistant Brand Manager** Melissa Joy Kong **Special Thanks to:** Christine Austin, Jeremy Biloon, Glenn Buonocore, Jim Childs, Rose Cirrincione, Jacqueline Fitzgerald, Carrie Frazier, Lauren Hall, Suzanne Janso, Brynn Joyce, Mona Li, Robert Marasco, Amy Migliaccio, Kimberly Posa, Richard Prue, Brooke Reger, Dave Rozzelle, Ilene Schreider, Adriana Tierno, Alex Voznesenskiy, Sydney Webber

Copyright © 2010
Time Home Entertainment Inc.
Published by Time Home Entertainment Inc.
135 West 50th Street New York, New York 10020

ISBN 10: 1-60320-146-7
ISBN 13: 978-1-60320-146-9
Library of Congress Control Number: 2010929872

We welcome your comments and suggestions about Time Home Entertainment Books. Please write to us at: Time Home Entertainment Inc., Attention: Book Editors, PO Box 11016, Des Moines, IA 50336-1016. If you would like to order any of our hardcover Collector's Edition books, please call us at 1-800-327-6388. (Monday through Friday, 7:00 a.m.–8:00 p.m. or Saturday, 7:00 a.m.–6:00 p.m. Central Time).

1 WCV 10

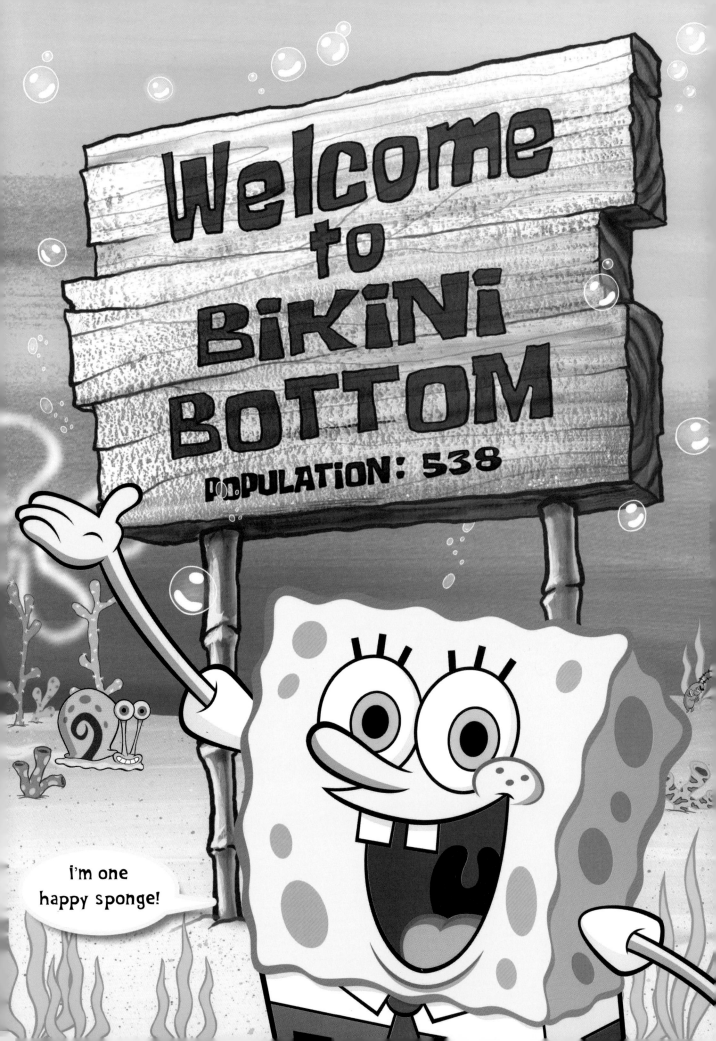

SAY HI TO SPONGEBOB

WELCOME, FANS!

Roll up, roll up! Welcome to the Bikini Bottom Undersea Showcase! And here is the star of the show ... SpongeBob SquarePants!

SpongeBob is a sea sponge who lives in the underwater town of Bikini Bottom. Although our porous friend works as a fry cook at the Krusty Krab restaurant by day, he is also a sponge of many talents.

GASP AT THE PERFECT PATTY-MAKING!

WONDER AT THE BRILLIANT BUBBLE-BLOWING!

PRESENTING . . .
PATRICK!

Starring opposite SpongeBob is his best friend, Patrick Star. Patrick spends his time contemplating difficult philosophical questions that have plagued the greatest minds since the dawn of time. Um, not really... Patrick doesn't actually think of anything much.

As you can see, Patrick is able to perform all sorts of emotions...

LOOK AT ME, I'M DANCING!

JOY

SADNESS

BEWILDERMENT

ALSO STARRING ...
SQUIDWARD!

Squidward Tentacles is SpongeBob's grouchy next-door neighbor. A rather unwilling co-star, Squidward dislikes a massive amount of things—and at the top of that list (although they don't realize it) are SpongeBob and Patrick!

I HATE ALL OF YOU.

HERE LIES SQUIDWARD'S HOPES AND DREAMS

However, Squidward is adept at **PERFORMING TRAGEDIES**

... and he loves **INTERPRETIVE DANCE** (the audience doesn't, though)

9

THE SUPPORTING CAST ...

GARY
Gary is SpongeBob's pet snail. He is a snail of few words (well, one word, actually). He knows how to please an audience, though— his party trick is tying shoelaces!

MR. KRABS
Mr. Krabs is the owner of the Krusty Krab restaurant, and is SpongeBob's boss. There's only one thing he likes... money! And the only thing he likes to spend it on is his whale of a daughter, Pearl.

MEOW!

THAT'S RIGHT, GARY HAS FEET!

GO, PEARL!

SANDY

Sandy Cheeks is Bikini Bottom's resident rodent and super stuntwoman—there's nothing she likes more than doing dangerous stuff. She also has a very special costume—a unique airsuit and helmet, so she can breathe underwater.

PLANKTON

Of course, every show needs its bad guy... Sheldon J. Plankton is out to steal the secret formula for the Krabby Patty. However, despite his college education, he hasn't yet managed to get it. He lives with Karen his computer wife, who has a Nag Chip installed in her.

YEE-HAW!

CLAM WRESTLING, TEXAS STYLE!

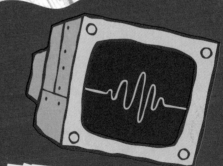

Who are you calling SMALL?

KAREN – A WIRED INTEGRATED FEMALE ELECTROENCEPHALOGRAPH

WACKY WORDS

Can you work out where all these Bikini Bottom characters fit into the grid? Check the box when you find each one.

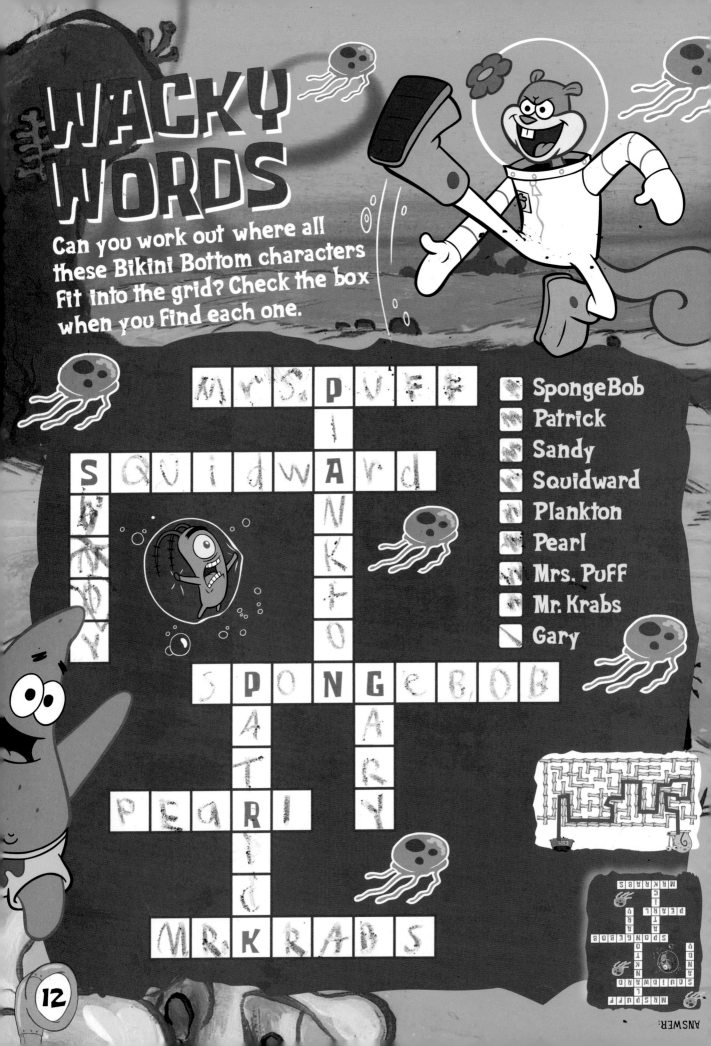

- [ ] SpongeBob
- [ ] Patrick
- [ ] Sandy
- [ ] Squidward
- [ ] Plankton
- [ ] Pearl
- [ ] Mrs. Puff
- [ ] Mr. Krabs
- [ ] Gary

MRS PUFF

SQUIDWARD

PLANKTON

SPONGEBOB

PEARL

PATRIC

GARY

MRKRABS

FOOD TRAIL

GARY

Gary is hungry! Help him get through the maze to find his food.

START

FINISH

ANSWER on page 12.

SPONGEBOB DIFFERENT PANTS

All these pictures of SpongeBob look the same—but they're not! Look closely and find the only two that match exactly.

1

2

3

4

5

6

SpongeBob SquareFace

crazy

scared

happy

and, when he's flipping those pretty patties...

love struck

Patrick, meanwhile, is...

Patrick

Draw and color in some more SpongeBob faces.

Design a new Bikini Bottomite to join the crew. Draw, color in and give him, her (or it) a name.

SpongeBob and Gary started out like this . . .

Audrey

Name ....

Jelly fishing. Bubble blowing. Riding on fishing hooks. SpongeBob and Patrick can always find reasons to be happy.

"To be happy as a clam," says SpongeBob, "you just have to . . ."

Think happy!

Hippy! Heppy! Happy!

How many times is the word **HAPPY** spelled out in the bubbles?

Draw a line through each one, then count them and write the number.

Happiness Is ...
a surprise present!

What do you give the sponge who has everything? **You decide!**
Draw and color in a surprise gift to make SpongeBob happy, and write your name on the gift tag.

To SpongeBob From

Jeray

Picture frome

PLANKTON'S PLANS

Sheldon J. Plankton has two goals in life: to steal the recipe for the Krabby Patty and to take over the world. So far, both have been unsuccessful. This corrupt copepod has tried everything to get his miniscule mitts on the secret formula . . .

BEING EVIL IS TOO MUCH FUN!

1 His first evil scheme was to take over SpongeBob's brain . . .

2 Then he tried to build a robotic Mr. Krabs . . .

3

He even changed places with Mr. Krabs by using Karen's "switch-lives-just-to-know-what-it's-like-o-mogrifier".

However, each and every one of his devious endeavors has been thwarted (often by an unwitting SpongeBob).

QUAKE IN FEAR, MORTAL FOOLS!

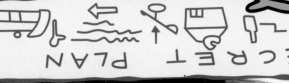

SECRET PLAN # 0422614132

Because of Plankton's numerous failures, the Chum Bucket remains the most unsuccessful business venture in Bikini Bottom, with a menu that couldn't tickle anyone's tastebuds. Can you take pity on poor Plankton and come up with a new item for the Chum Bucket's menu? Draw your idea in the space below!

PLANKTON'S PERPLEXING PUZZLES

Can you find all of Plankton's favorite words in the grid? Words can run forwards, backwards, up, down and diagonally.

KNOWLEDGE IS POWER!

You can tell he went to college!

BAD
CATASTROPHIC
CORRUPT
CUNNING
DEMENTED

DEPRAVED
DERANGED
DESTRUCTIVE
DIABOLICAL
EVIL

INSANE
MALEVOLENT
MANIACAL
MEAN
NASTY

PSYCHOTIC
VILLAINOUS
WICKED
ZEALOUS

E	J	S	E	Y	I	Y	D	F	T	L	L	L	Q	D
D	V	U	P	N	T	E	X	N	Q	A	A	I	B	X
C	E	I	S	S	P	S	E	M	N	C	C	V	W	M
P	U	A	T	R	Y	L	A	A	Z	I	A	E	J	O
F	N	N	A	C	O	C	E	N	V	L	I	V	H	N
E	M	V	N	V	U	M	H	N	O	O	N	E	Z	R
V	E	H	E	I	F	R	C	O	E	B	A	Q	E	I
D	N	L	V	Z	N	K	T	Z	T	A	M	D	A	H
J	A	N	J	M	B	G	S	S	B	I	S	E	L	P
M	D	E	G	N	A	R	E	D	E	D	C	M	O	Q
V	I	L	L	A	I	N	O	U	S	D	C	E	U	N
C	O	R	R	U	P	T	B	A	D	T	X	N	S	J
D	E	K	C	I	W	U	A	A	C	I	I	T	N	S
O	T	D	S	L	S	L	B	R	O	V	Q	E	C	X
C	I	H	P	O	R	T	S	A	T	A	C	D	H	C

Answer:

20

Draw lines to match the members of Plankton's family into pairs.

Which line will lead Plankton to the Krabby Patty?

HE'LL NEVER GET THE FORMULA, YOU KNOW . . .
1
2
3
4

Answer: Line 3 leads to the Krabby Patty.

SUPER SPOT

Here comes SuperSponge—soaking up crime with his faithful sidekick. These crime scenes look the same, but 15 things are different in picture 2. Can you spot them all?

Put on your superhero cape and help find the hiding places of **8** of the Plankton clan. You might need this, too!

You found all **8?** Then here's your SpongeBob superhero badge. Color it in—and wear with pride!

Bikini Bottom

Up Close

Let's take a look around the undersea city ...

124 Conch Street is the two-bedroom pineapple house that yellow sea sponge **SpongeBob SquarePants** calls home. He shares it with his pet snail, **Gary**.

SpongeBob's dream is to pass his boat driving test at Mrs. Puff's Boating School, but he has failed it **1,258,056** times. In one desperate try to get his license, SpongeBob had a walkie-talkie planted in his head so that his friend Patrick could guide him in secret. But he still failed ...

Meow!

What does SpongeBob lift to keep fit?
Check ✓ the correct answer.

a

b

c

A pink starfish called **Patrick Star** lives under a rock at 120 Conch Street.

On Best Friends' Day, Patrick gave SpongeBob his most prized possession: an enormous ball of **chewing gum.** Used chewing gum. Complete with moldy pizza and a smelly sock.

Hey, that's what friends are for!

Go away! I don't like you!

A miserable octopus called **Squidward Tentacles** lives at 122 Conch Street, in Tiki Head House.

Squidward plays (bad) clarinet with the Bikini Bottom Orchestra and is not very friendly ...

Patrick Star
Rock

Conch Street
Bikini Bottom

Squidward Tentacles
Tiki Head House

Conch Street
Bikini Bottom

Write house numbers to complete the addresses.

AROUND BIKINI BOTTOM

The underwater town of Bikini Bottom is a treasure trove of watery wonder. Let's take a look around!

Mrs. Puff's Boating School
SpongeBob's taken her class many times—but sadly still doesn't have his driver's license.

Conch Street
A quiet, residential street. Well, it would be if it didn't have SpongeBob and Patrick living on it!

Anchor House
Mr. Krabs and Pearl reside in this eccentrically shaped abode.

The Krusty Krab

The finest eating establishment ever established for eating! (According to Mr. Krabs at least ...)

Jellyfish Fields

In jellyfishing season, this place is swarming with these scrummy critters—catch them if you can!

Goo Lagoon

The local beach, where Larry the Lobster keeps a lookout.

The Chum Bucket

The food in Plankton's restaurant is so bad that nobody ever goes there. If only Plankton could get his hands on that Krabby Patty recipe...

Around Town

The Anchor House is where Mr. Eugene Krabs lives with his whale-of-a-daughter, Pearl. Mr. Krabs loves money ... making money, stroking money, stacking money, sorting money, hiding money, saving money, smelling money, counting money. What he doesn't like is spending it!

When SpongeBob gave Mr. Krabs a new mattress and got rid of the old one, he fainted, because all his money was hidden in it!

Help Mr. Krabs count his money. Write a total in each box.

12

The Treedome is where karate-kicking, all-action Texan squirrel **Sandy Cheeks** lives.

SpongeBob has a huge crush on Sandy, and he's always trying to impress her. When Sandy helped SpongeBob train for the Mussel Beach body building event, SpongeBob thought all that exercise was too much—so he bought a pair of fake muscle arms to wear.

Yee-haw!

True or False?
Check ✓ or cross ✗ each fact.

b **Sandy is from Tahiti.** ✗

a **Sandy is a gerbil.**

c **SpongeBob loves Sandy.** ✓

ANSWERS: 1. False she's a squirrel. 2. False she's from Texas. 3. True he sure does!

Krusty Krab versus

The **Krusty Krab** is Mr. Krabs' lobster pot fast-food joint.

SpongeBob works there as a fry cook, flipping hundreds of the top-secret-recipe Krabby Patties that have made Mr. Krabs a very rich crustacean.

SpongeBob loves his job so much that when he was **1 minute** late one morning he moved in to the Krusty Krab so it wouldn't happen again.

it's me pleasure to take yer money!

TODAY'S SPECIALS

AsE _ _ _ _ SODAS

YUKRST _ _ _ _ _ _ KELP

HSIF _ _ _ _ FRIES

Unscramble the white letters to complete the Krusty Krab specials menu.

ANSWERS: The specials are: SEA SODAS, KRUSTY KELP and FISH FRIES.

Chum Bucket

Sheldon Plankton is the mean, green and microscopic owner of the **Chum Bucket**, the worst eating place in the world. Plankton's only hope of attracting customers is to steal Mr. Krabs' Krabby Patty recipe, and this is what he plans to do, aided by his huge family.

Once, Plankton hid out in SpongeBob's head and took control of his **brain.** It took a sponge of unusual sponginess to withstand handing over the secret recipe . . .

How many of the Plankton clan can you spot in this picture? Write the number.

7

ANSWER: There are 7 of Plankton's relatives.

AT WORK WITH SPONGEBOB

Welcome to the Krusty Krab— the finest eating establishment ever established for eating!

This is where I work as the trusted fry cook. Sometimes Mr. Krabs is even kind enough to give me double overtime—he's the best boss a sponge could ask for! Come on, let me show you around . . .

Mr. Krabs is the owner of the restaurant. This kindly crustacean always puts the customers first.

Ketchup packets

State-of-the-art condiment dispenser units

This is the kitchen, where I work my magic. To make the perfect Krabby Patty, grill the Patty at exactly 298 degrees Fahrenheit. Then put the Patty on the bun, add lettuce, cheese, onion, tomato, ketchup, mustard and pickles. Dee-licious!

The spatula
An advanced patty-control mechanism

Ice cubes
Imported high-quality temperature devices

Cash register
An automated money-handling system

GIVE ME A BREAK!

Let me introduce my esteemed colleague, Squidward. Squidward works as a cashier. He loves working here almost as much as I do—he always has a spring in his step and a song in his heart.

PUZZLED WITH PATRICK

Hi! Do you wanna test your brain to the limit? Push it harder than it's ever been pushed before? Well get ready, because these puzzles are even more difficult than spelling ... difficult!

Connect the dots to find out what the picture is!

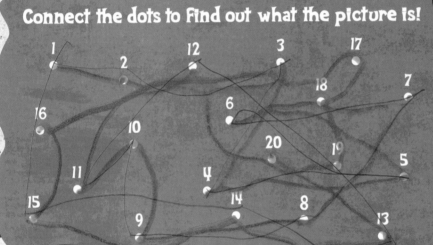

1 2 12 3 17
16 18 7
6
10 20 19 5
11 4
15 14 8 13
9

I KNOW WHAT IT IS ... A MESS!

SpongeBob and I are playing hide and seek. Can you find us?

I'm behind the sofa and SpongeBob is in the kitchen.

Patrick, if I had one dollar for every brain you don't have, I'd have one dollar.

I just don't know which way to go!

Can you help me find the way through the maze to get to my beloved ice cream?

That's easy!

This is an echinoderm. Read the word then cover it up. How do you spell it?

IT

Can you unscramble the letters to reveal someone from Bikini Bottom?

Hmm . . . well if it's not Plank, who could it be?

NOTPLANK

Use the code to color in the picture and see an amazing underwater scene!

= 1
= 2
= 3
= 4

That's right, it's SpongeBob's house! But all the lights are turned off.

AMAZING MAZE

Avast, me hearties! SpongeBob and Patrick are searching for lost treasure. Find the path through the maze—but be quick, or it'll be the plank for you!

SPONGEBOB PIRATEPANTS

Color in this swashbuckling picture and design your own Bikini Bottom pirate flag, too!

CURSES UPON YE!

Shopkin

tootie Bread

WRITE IN YOUR PIRATE NAME Arr...m-e...jer

39

Spot the Difference

These pictures look the same, but 10 things are different in picture 2. Can you spot them all?

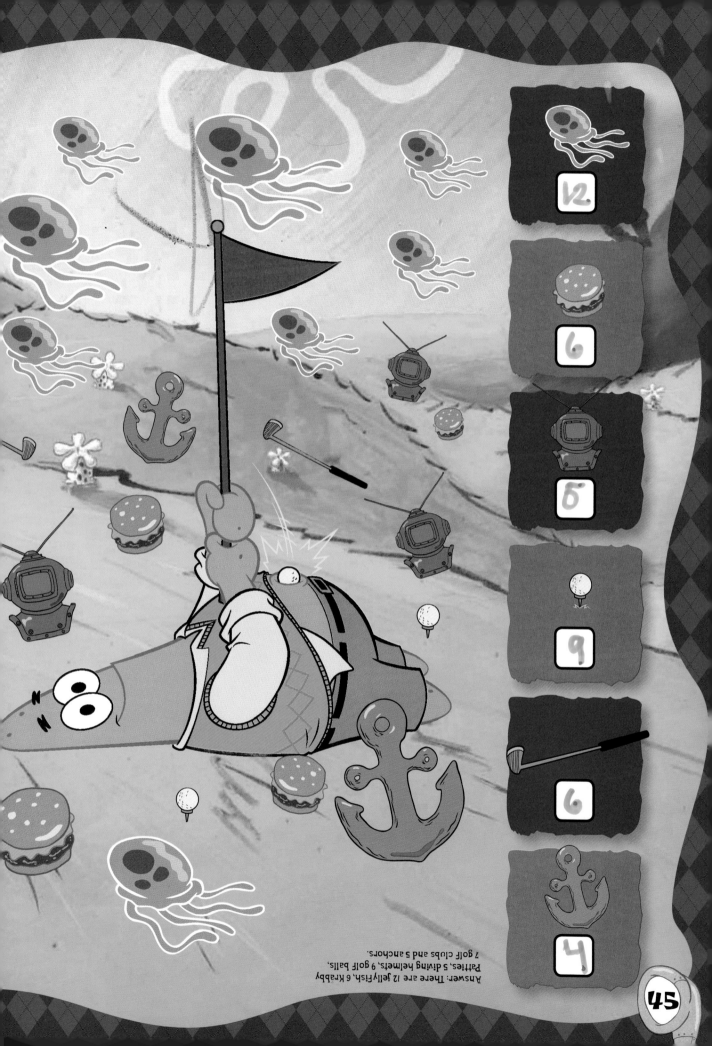

Attack of the Sticky Notes

Help!
Get 'em off me!

In Bikini Bottom there's a disaster waiting around every sea corner, and SpongeBob always finds it. Today it's a sticky note attack!

Decorate all the sticky notes on SpongeBob, then count and write the total in the box.

There are 12 sticky notes

THE BEST DAY EVER

It doesn't take much to keep SpongeBob as happy as a clam, as you can see from his BEST DAY EVER list.

Write your name and things that make you happy on your own BEST DAY EVER list.

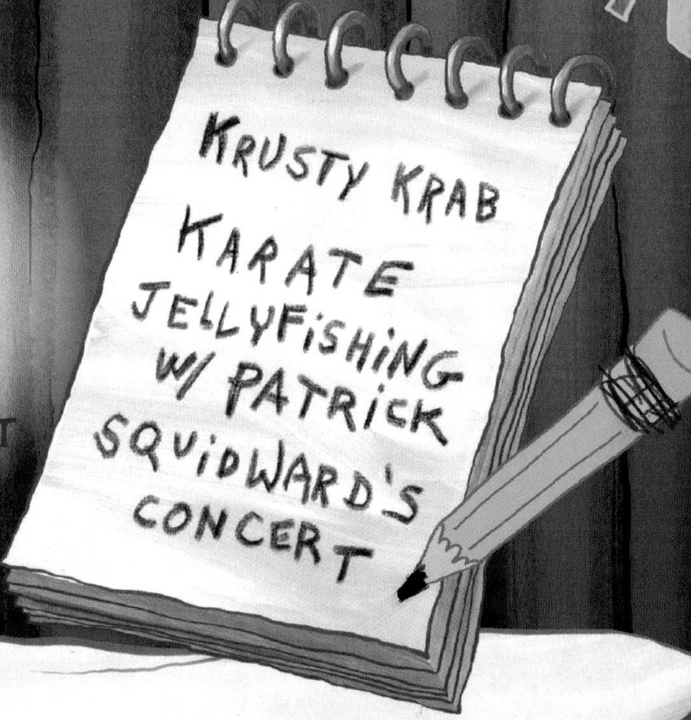

KRUSTY KRAB
KARATE
JELLYFISHING W/ PATRICK
SQUIDWARD'S CONCERT

My BEST DAY EVER list

NAME: Jerzey

1. go shopping for toys
2. go to Australia
3. 95 hor rtub
4.

DRAW PATRICK

Grab a pencil and follow these six simple steps!

YOU'RE A WORK OF ART ALREADY, PATRICK!

1 Draw a boomerang shape on a piece of paper.

2 Draw a pear shape over the top.

3 Draw a cross through the middle, then add some legs.

4 Give him eyes above the line on either side. Add a mouth below.

5 Carefully erase the lines. Add eyebrows and a belly button.

6 He's naked! Quickly draw on a pair of patterned shorts.

EVEN I COULD DO IT! MAYBE . . .

FINISH IT SHARPISH—THEN BACK TO WORK!

CRAZY CROSSWORD

Have a go at this spectacular Bikini Bottom crossword!

ACROSS

4 Bikini Bottom's beach (3, 6)

7 Mr. Krabs' favorite thing (5)

10 SpongeBob lives in a _____ under the sea (9)

11 The shape of SpongeBob's pants (6)

12 The instrument that Squidward plays—badly! (8)

14 Plankton's first name (7)

15 Plankton's restaurant is the _____ Bucket (4)

16 The name of Plankton's computer wife (5)

DOWN

1 SpongeBob's favorite cooking utensil (7)

2 Squidward's last name (9)

3 The Krusty Krab's specialty (6, 5)

5 The only thing Gary says (4)

6 Where Sandy comes from—yee-haw! (5)

8 What SpongeBob and Patrick like to catch in nets (9)

9 SpongeBob's job at the Krusty Krab (3, 4)

13 Mr. Krabs' whale of a daughter (5)

GO WEST!

SpongeBob RanchPants and Sheriff Star are on patrol! Look at the picture and try to spot the matching shadow.

HOWDY, PARTNER!

Answer: E is the correct shadow

IN A TANGLE

Yee-haw! SpongeBob is all dressed up
and ready For a Wild West adventure!
He just needs his trusty steed, Mystery.
Which line will lead him to Mystery?

1 2 3 4

I'M NUTS
ABOUT
COWBOYS!

PUZZLED WITH PATRICK

Wow, you're back for more? Looks like you really love doing hard stuff, so have a go at these. But watch out, they're tougher than a clam's shell!

MY BRAIN HURTS!

Which line will lead SpongeBob to the Krabby Patty?

4
3
1 2

Look at the pictures and find the one that's different.

IT'S D! SQUIDWARD'S GONE OUT SHOPPING. IN ALL THE OTHERS HE'S IN THE KITCHEN.

A   B   C   D   E

Can you spot me in this picture?

I'LL GIVE YOU A CLUE—I'M IN DISGUISE.

You can draw SpongeBob! Here's how ...

1

Draw a rectangle.

2

Draw SpongeBob's Face on it.

YOU'RE AN ARTIST!

Which is the odd one out?

WELL, I NEVER TRIED WEARING A TIE ...

WOW, IT'S A GIRAFFE!

SpongeBob's blowing a bubble. What shape is it?

SPONGEY Secrets

Here are some of SpongeBob's most top-secret secrets. But a word is missing from each one.

Choose the correct word from the opposite page to complete each secret, and write the number in each porthole.

To earn some extra cash, SpongeBob sold ...

door to door.

SpongeBob likes to put ...

on both sides of his toast.

At the zoo, SpongeBob made an oyster cry when he tossed a ...

OYSTER STADIUM

BIKINI BOTTOM ZOO

at it.

1 jellyfish jelly

2 chocolate bars

4 Ol' Buzzy

5 Gary

3 squirrels

6 peanut

7 pickle

a SpongeBob called his favorite jellyfish . . .

SpongeBob went on strike when a customer said there was no . . .

on his Krabby Patty.

SpongeBob became a comedy star when he told jokes about . . .

f SpongeBob was taught to tie his shoelaces by . . .

ANSWERS: a–2 b–1 c–6 d–4 e–7 f–5 g–3

59

Help Patrick count how many new colored lights he needs to buy.

bulbs

Puzzled with Patrick

Want to work your brain cells harder than you've ever worked them before? Well, prepare for Patrick's puzzles!

Safe

Where does Mr. Krabs keep the secret Krabby Patty recipe book?

SECRET RECIPE FOR A KRABBY PATTY

It's in SpongeBob's head.

Souvenir

Color in the shapes with a spot and see what's left. Think you know what the mystery object is?

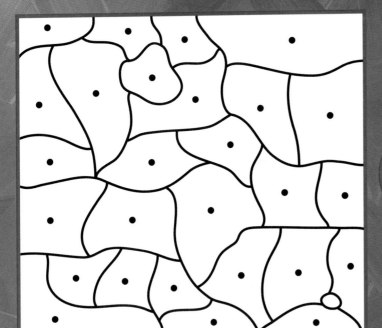

It's the grain of sand I brought back from Mussel Beach.

Jack Kahuna Laguna

Where would you find ace surfer JKL?

Easy. ABCDEFGHI . . . JKL!

The Perfect Krabby Patty

Which one is it?

The one that smells good?

Rock

Color in the picture using the code.

KEY

1 □

1

Huh?

SMILE, PLEASE!

SpongeBob is really snap-happy since he got his new camera. But it has its own mind when it comes to what pictures to take—often clicking away before Sponge-Bob has had a chance to say "cheese!" The results are, well, see for yourself . . .

Help SpongeBob match these photos of his friends to their name labels.

Plankton

a

Patrick

b

Squidward

It sure was hard to get Gary to come out of his shell!

e

d

Mrs. Puff

Don't give up the day job!

SpongeB____ ____ ____ aren't exactly perfect. Do you know ____ ____ job he does each day? Check the box.

☐ lif____ ☐ ____ ☐ Fry cook

Mr. Kr____

Gary

Sandy

Pearl

Hate
saDNESS
DEWiLDERment
crying

EXITing

e

f

g

h

AlphaBob LetterPants

Write your name, initials or a word in AlphaBob letters. Favorites are smile, happy and, you guessed it, spongey!

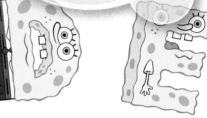

Curse that supple sponge!

It takes a sea sponge of superior squeeziness, squelchiness and squishiness to squidge himself into the letters of the alphabet. SpongeBob is that sponge.

Happiness

Copy the colored letter into the porthole by each SpongeFact, then rearrange them into a spongey saying.

Aaargh! What have I done?

When Squidward looked after SpongeBob's pet snail, it became ill. When SpongeBob came home he took the snail medicine meant for Gary and turned into ... **S**pongeSnail.

SpongeBob ate some **O**nion ice cream, and people started to avoid him because of his stinky breath. When Patrick said it was maybe because he was ugly, SpongeBob took to wearing a disguise ...

When SpongeBob StarPants hit the big time in a **T**V ad for the Krusty Krab, he believed he'd quit his job. But when his fans only wanted to see him flipping patties, it was back to work.

When Pearl the **W**hale needed a date for the Poseidon Elementary school prom, SpongeBob tried to make himself tall, dark and handsome. Not easy for someone short, square and yellow ...

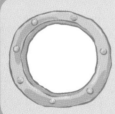

SpongeBob trained **G**ary to race against Snelle, Squidward's super-snail. But both trailed home in a race won by Patrick's entry ... a racing rock.

When SpongeBob had to write an **E**ssay he stayed up all night. He began seeing things—then that's what ended up in his essay.

The title SpongeBob craves is **E**mployee of the Month. He puts in long hours for almost no pay to earn the honor . . . and the cake.

Poo-eeee!

Patrick was the only Bikini Bottomite without a **N**ose, so he got one. He liked it—until he found that there were bad smells as well as good ones.

Once, a customer accused SpongeBob of **F**orgetting to put **P**ickles on a Krabby Patty. He was so upset that he quit, but when business slowed down, Mr. Krabs begged him to come back.

Happiness is a

_____ _____ !

Puzzled with Patrick

Patrick loves puzzle stuff, but he's not much good at puzzle stuff, so can you help?

Prize Photo
This photo won First Prize at the Bikini Bottom Camera Club Show.
Can you guess the title?

Patrick (hey, that's me!)
As Seen from Pluto.

Spelling Bee
Which word is always spelt wrongly?

is it
r-o-n-g-l-y?

How Long...
is a piece of string?

Errrr?

Let's Rock!

Far out! Which shadow matches the rockin' rockers?

a

b

c

d

72

Answer: Shadow d.

Best Buddies

One picture is different from the rest. Can you spot the odd one out?

Answer: E is the odd one out: SpongeBob's tie is blue.

Now Leaving ...

You are now leaving Bikini Bottom—once you find your way through the seaweed maze!

Byeee!

Now Leaving BIKINI BOTTOM

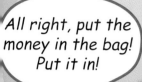

QUESTION TIME

Ahoy, landlubbers! Test your nautical knowledge with this crazy quiz!

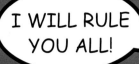

I WILL RULE YOU ALL!

4

What does Plankton want the recipe for?

g) The Triple Gooberberry Surprise

h) The Krabby Patty

1

Whose favorite activities include clam wrestling and karate?

a) Sandy

b) Squidward

5

What is Squidward's job at the Krusty Krab?

i) Cashier

j) Dishwasher

2

What is Patrick's last name?

c) Star

d) Sea

6

What is Mr. Krabs' favorite thing?

k) Money

l) Honey

3

What is the name of SpongeBob's street?

e) Conch Street

f) Perch Street

7

What does Squidward call his beloved clarinet?

m) Clary

n) Netty

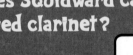

8 Who is the lifeguard at Goo Lagoon?
o) Gary
p) Larry

VERY IMPRESSIVE ... FOR A MORON.

11 What shape is Mr. Krabs' house?
u) An anchor
v) A ship

9 What is Gary's special talent?
q) Knitting scarves
r) Tying shoelaces

12 Who are Bikini Bottom's resident superheroes?
w) Mermaid Man and Barnacle Boy
x) Mollusk Man and Blowfish Boy

10 What is the name of Plankton's wife?
s) Katherine
t) Karen

13 Who is SpongeBob's driving instructor?
y) Mrs. Huff
z) Mrs. Puff

Now write in the correct letter for each number and reveal the answer to this question:

WHO IS GARY'S COUSIN?

8   1   10   9   5   2   6

Answers: 1 Sandy (a) 2 Star (c) 3 Conch Street (e) 4 The Krabby Patty (h) 5 Cashier (t) 6 Money (k) 7 Clary (m) 8 Larry (p) 9 Tying shoelaces (r) 10 Karen (t) 11 An anchor (u) 12 Mermaid Man and Barnacle Boy (w) 13 Mrs. Puff (z). Patrick is Gary's cousin.

Byeee!

Crack SpongeBob's coded message by writing the letter for each symbol.

78